P9-BJX-491

Contrary Bear

by Phyllis Root
pictures by Laura Cornell

A Laura Geringer Book

An Imprint of HarperCollinsPublishers

Library of Congress Cataloging-in-Publication Data
Root, Phyllis.
    Contrary bear / by Phyllis Root ; pictures by Laura Cornell.
        p.   cm.
    Summary: After she sees how upset her father has become, a little girl who blames her
bad behavior on her stuffed bear tells her father that the bear will try to act better.
    ISBN 0-06-025085-2. — ISBN 0-06-025086-0 (lib. bdg.)
    [1. Behavior—Fiction.   2. Toys—Fiction.   3. Fathers and daughters—Fiction.]
I. Cornell, Laura, ill.   II. Title.
PZ7.R6784Cm 1996   95-31644
[E]—dc20   CIP
                                                                                    AC

Typography by Christine Kettner
1   2   3   4   5   6   7   8   9   10
❖
First Edition

For Amelia, my first Contrary Bear, and Contrary Bears everywhere—P.R.

For Laura and Caitlyn—L.C.

Bear is my best friend. We do everything together. Dad calls him Contrary Bear. That's because Bear doesn't always do what he's supposed to do.

"Put on your shoes, please," Dad said when Bear and I wanted to go out to play.

"I want them off," said Contrary Bear.

"On, please," said Dad.

"Off," said Bear.

"On," said Dad, and he tied the laces twice.

Contrary Bear was so mad he stomped
around the living room three times.

Bear and I were building a sand fortress when Jimmy came over to play.

"I'll dig the moat around the edge," he said.

So I gave him my yellow shovel.

Jimmy dug the moat right into the tower and knocked it over. Bear didn't mean to throw sand.

But he did.

"I think you'd better come into the house,"
Dad said.

"I want to stay out," said Contrary Bear.

"In," said Dad.

"Out," said Bear.

"In."

"Out."

Dad picked me up and carried me into the
house. Bear came, too, but he made a face.

"Bear wants me to read him a story," I told Dad at naptime.

"You can read one if you're quiet about it," Dad said.

So I read him the quiet part. But when I got to the train part, Contrary Bear said, "Make a noise like a whistle."

"*Too whoo whoo*," I hollered.

Dad came running in.

"It's a train," said Contrary Bear. "It has to be noisy."

"This train will have to be quiet," Dad said.

"Noisy," said Bear.

"Quiet," said Dad.

"Too whoo whoo," yelled Bear.

Dad took the book away and shut the door.

Dad was in the kitchen when Bear and I got up from our nap.

"May Bear and I please have a piece of carrot cake?" I asked.

"Just a little one," he answered. "We're going to eat soon."

"I want a big piece," said Contrary Bear.

"Little," said Dad.

"Big," said Bear.

Dad cut a tiny piece of carrot cake. You could hardly see it, it was so small. Bear threw it on the floor.

"All right," said Dad. "I can see you're not very hungry."

So Bear and I did not get any cake until after supper.

Bear sat on the edge of the tub to watch me take my bath.

"Now don't splash water," Dad said. "I want that bear to stay dry."

"Wet!" cried Contrary Bear after Dad left.

He jumped in the tub with a big splash.
"Wet, wet, wet!"

"I told you to keep that bear dry!" Dad
yelled when he came back in.

"That does it," Dad said. "No more bath, no more Bear." He pulled the plug and hung Bear up to dry. Then he pulled my nightgown over my head without even drying me off.

"Dad's pretty mad," I told Bear.

Bear didn't say anything.

"Maybe tomorrow you could try harder to behave," I said.

"Take me down," said Bear.

"Dad," I hollered. "Bear wants to come down."

"That's too bad," Dad called back.

"He says he doesn't mean to be contrary," I yelled.

Dad came to the bathroom door.

"What do you think we could do about that?" he asked.

"Bear says if you take him down, he'll try harder to be good tomorrow," I said.

So Dad took Bear down.

Thunk-a-thunk-a-thunk went Bear in the clothes dryer.

When Bear was warm and dry, Dad tucked him into bed.

"Sometimes Bear likes a bedtime hug," I told Dad.

"Sometimes I do, too," Dad said. He hugged Bear and me and gave us both an extra kiss.

"Be quiet now and go to sleep," he said as he turned out the light.

"Tell me a bedtime story," Bear whispered in my ear. "A quiet one."

"Once upon a time," I whispered back, "there was a very quiet train. *Chug-a-chug-a-chug, sh-sh-shhhhhh . . .*"